Sister was breathing hard and almost ready to cry. She looked just the way Barry had looked the day before.

"I've been ROBBED!" she cried.

Barry's mouth fell open. "You *too?* What did they take?"

"My Bear Scout flashlight! I brought it in for show and tell this afternoon and left it in my locker. And when I went to put my books away at lunchtime, it was gone!"

BIG CHAPTER BOOKS

The Berenstain Bears and the Drug Free Zone

The Berenstain Bears and the New Girl in Town

The Berenstain Bears Gotta Dance!

The Berenstain Bears and the Nerdy Nephew

The Berenstain Bears Accept No Substitutes

The Berenstain Bears and the Female Fullback

The Berenstain Bears and the Red-Handed Thief

The Berenstain Bears
and the Wheelchair Commando

Coming Soon

The Berenstain Bears and the School Scandal Sheet

The Berenstain Bears at Camp Crush

The Berenstain Bears
and the Galloping Ghost

The Berenstain Bears
and the
RED-HANDED THIEF

by Stan & Jan Berenstain

A BIG CHAPTER BOOK™

Random House 🏠 New York

Copyright © 1993 by Berenstain Enterprises, Inc.
All rights reserved under International and Pan-American Copyright
Conventions. Published in the United States by Random House, Inc.,
New York, and simultaneously in Canada by Random House of
Canada Limited, Toronto.

Library of Congress Cataloging-in-Publication Data
Berenstain, Stan.
The Berenstain Bears and the red-handed thief /
by Stan and Jan Berenstain.
   p.   cm. — (A Big chapter book)
SUMMARY: Mr. Dweebish, the new teacher at the Bear Country
School, tries to explain to the class bully how democracy works.
ISBN 0-679-84033-8 (pbk.) — ISBN 0-679-94033-2 (lib. bdg.)
[1. Democracy—Fiction. 2. Bullies—Fiction.   3. Schools—Fiction.
4. Teachers—Fiction.   5. Bears—Fiction.]   I. Berenstain, Jan.
II. Title.   III. Series: Berenstain, Stan.   Big chapter book.
PZ7.B4483Bejr   1993
[E]—dc20   93-8870

Manufactured in the United States of America   10 9 8 7 6 5 4 3 2 1

BIG CHAPTER BOOKS is a trademark of Berenstain Enterprises, Inc.

Contents

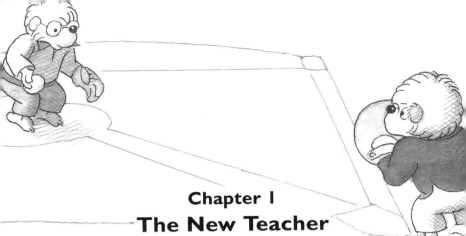

Chapter 1
The New Teacher

Rumors were as much a part of Bear Country School as walls and windows, bells and buzzers, homework and report cards. There were rumors about Too-Tall maybe getting suspended for his latest prank. There were rumors about a longer school day. There were rumors about almost anything. The latest rumor was about a new teacher coming to the school.

"What's the new teacher's name?" Brother Bear called to Cousin Freddy. They were playing catch after school on the school's baseball field. Brother crouched at home plate. His catcher's mitt was ready. Freddy wound up for the next pitch. WHACK. Freddy's fastball landed in Brother's mitt.

"Don't know," said Freddy.

"Strike one," said Brother. He threw the ball back to Freddy and signaled for a curveball. "Well, is the new teacher a grade teacher or some kind of special teacher?" he asked.

SMACK. Freddy's curveball zipped across home plate into Brother's mitt. "Don't know," called Freddy.

"Strike two," said Brother. He signaled for a slider. "Well, is it a man or a woman?" he asked.

"Don't know." POP.

"Strike three!" cried Brother. "You're out, Freddy."

"What do you mean, *I'm* out?" yelled

Freddy. "The *batter's* out!"

"No, *you're* out," said Brother. He tossed the ball back. "I asked you three easy questions about the new teacher, and you missed every one. Three strikes and you're out. What's with you, Freddy? You usually know everything that's going on in school."

Freddy shrugged.

Just then Sister Bear came running toward the baseball diamond. She stopped beside Brother at home plate and waved to Freddy to come over. She seemed very excited. "Hey, guys," she said. "I've got all the info on the new teacher!"

"Name?" asked Brother.

"Mr. Dweebish," said Sister.

"Grade or special?" asked Freddy.

"Special."

"Subject?" asked Brother.

"Social studies," answered Sister.

"Ugh!" Freddy groaned. "Another social studies teacher! They're all the same."

"Yeah, all boring," said Brother.

"Not Mr. Dweebish," said Sister.

"Another rumor," said Brother. "I can feel myself falling asleep in class already."

"No rumor!" said Sister. "This is straight from Teacher Jane. And she should know. Mr. Dweebish is from Bear Country University, and he's here to teach a special class. It's an experiment for just one hour a day in just one of the classes. If it works, Mr. Dweebish will teach one hour a day in *all* the classes next year."

"And what's the name of this special class?" asked Freddy.

Sister thought for a moment. "Uh...something about democracy," she said. "It's called...Formations of Democracy. I think."

"Formations?" said Freddy. He made a face. "Sounds more like fighter planes."

"Or football," said Brother.

"Or stalactites and stalagmites," said Freddy.

"Okay, okay," said Sister. "So it's not 'formations.' But it sounds like 'formations.'"

"Creations?" said Freddy. "Constellations? Vibrations?"

"Vibrations of Democracy?" groaned Brother. "Gimme a break!"

"It's like building houses," said Sister. She was thinking very hard.

"Foundations?" asked Brother.

"That's it!" cried Sister. "Foundations of Democracy!"

"Sounds boring to me," said Brother. "And which is the lucky class that gets an hour a day with this Dweebish?"

Sister grinned. "Guess."

"Oh no," moaned Brother.

"Yep," said Sister. "Teacher Bob's class! Congratulations."

"Thanks," said Brother. "And congratulations to you, Sis, for getting to miss it."

"Oh, but I think it will be interesting," said Sister. "And I won't miss it, either."

"What do you mean?" said Freddy. "You're not in our class. You're in Teacher Jane's class."

"And that's exactly why Teacher Jane was just telling me all about Mr. Dweebish," said Sister. "She chose me and Lizzy Bruin as honors social studies students. For one hour each day, we get to move up to your class for Formations of Democracy."

"Foundations," said Brother.

"Whatever," said Sister. "Gimme the ball, Freddy. I want to throw a couple."

"Say 'please,'" said Freddy.

"Please," said Sister.

"Say 'pretty please,'" said Freddy.

"Pretty please."

"Say 'pretty please with sugar on top.'"

"Pretty please with a baseball bat on top of your head," said Sister.

"Okay, okay," said Freddy. He handed Sister the ball. "Don't get upset."

Sister hurried out to the pitcher's mound while Brother handed Freddy his catcher's mitt. "You catch her," Brother said. "My hand's tired." Brother knew something Freddy didn't know. Maybe Sister was two years younger and a girl. But she had one of the hardest fastballs at Bear Country School. "Better signal for a curveball," Brother told Freddy.

Freddy looked up. "Why?"

"Trust me," said Brother.

Freddy shrugged and put down two fingers for a curveball. Sister read the sign and wound up. The pitch came at Freddy like a rocket. It slammed into his mitt. CRACK!

"Yow!" cried Freddy. He dropped both the ball and the catcher's mitt. Then he started jumping up and down on home plate, shaking his hand. "I signaled for a curveball!" he screamed at Sister.

"I guess the sun was in my eyes," said Sister with a grin. "Sorry about that. Well, gotta go. I want to tell Mama and Papa about Formations of Democracy."

"Foundations," said Brother.

But Sister was already heading home. She was running at top speed.

Brother looked at Freddy. "My little sister can be a real pain in the neck," he said.

"You mean pain in the hand," said Freddy, moaning.

Brother laughed. "Not a bad fastball, though," he said.

But Freddy had forgotten all about Sister's fastball and his aching hand. He was looking toward the parking lot at the other side of the school grounds. A car he had never seen before was pulling into a space in the teachers' section. "Look over there," he said.

Brother and Freddy both turned to get a good look. The driver got out of the car and walked toward the school. Mr. Honeycomb, the principal, was waiting to greet him.

"Must be Mr. Dweebish, the new teacher," said Freddy.

"Must be," said Brother.

The new teacher wore a gray hat, a gray suit, and thick glasses that glinted in the afternoon sun. He was almost a head shorter than Mr. Honeycomb. And he was rather roly-poly.

"He kind of looks like his name," said Brother.

"And let's not forget nerdish and wimp-ish," said Freddy. "What do you think?"

Brother sighed. "I think Too-Tall and his gang will eat him alive."

Chapter 2
The Dweebish Hour

The very next day, before lunch, Teacher Bob told the cubs that a new daily social studies class was about to begin. He also said that Sister Bear and Lizzy Bruin would be joining them from Teacher Jane's class.

The buzzing of cub voices stopped the moment the new teacher entered the room. Mr. Dweebish went straight to the blackboard and wrote his name on it. There were a few giggles. "I told you he'd be a dweeb," whispered Too-Tall Grizzly to Skuzz just loud enough for everyone to hear. More giggles could be heard.

Mr. Dweebish pretended not to notice. Under his name on the blackboard, he wrote "Foundations of Democracy." Then he turned to the class. "What are foundations?" he asked in a loud clear voice. He wore thick glasses. Behind them his eyes were bright and interested.

The cubs looked at each other. They had expected some kind of opening talk by the new teacher telling them what "Foundations of Democracy" meant. This new teacher was different. He jumped right into things!

Sister Bear's hand went up. She was frowning the way she always did when she thought hard about something. Mr. Dweebish saw right away that Sister was younger than the other cubs in class. "You must be one of the honors students from Teacher Jane's class," he said.

"Yes," said Sister. "My name is Sister Bear."

"Well, Sister, what are foundations?"

"They're like what you build a house on top of," said Sister.

Most of the class laughed. "Some honors student," cracked Too-Tall.

THEY'RE LIKE WHAT YOU BUILD A HOUSE ON TOP OF.

SOME HONORS STUDENT.

Mr. Dweebish glanced at Too-Tall with a cold smile and said, "Actually, Sister is right. Foundations are exactly like what you build houses on. They're what come first when you build anything. And that could be anything from a house to a political system. But the foundations of democracy aren't bricks and concrete. They're ideas and activities. What do you think of first when you think of democracy?"

After a moment, Cousin Freddy raised his hand and was called on. "Voting," he said.

"Very good," said Mr. Dweebish. "Voting is an activity that is a foundation of democracy. And what idea is it based on?"

Queenie McBear raised her hand. "Representation!"

"Exactly," said Mr. Dweebish. "In a democracy, the people get to decide who represents them in government. They decide who will run their country and make their laws. And it is usually the majority of people who get their way."

"Then I'm the majority in my gang," said Too-Tall loudly without raising his hand. "Because I *always* get my way!"

"Oh, shut up, Too-Tall," said Bertha Bruin.

"Yeah, stop being such a creep," said Babs Bruno.

"Calm down, class," said Mr. Dweebish. He looked straight at Too-Tall through his thick glasses. "Too-Tall," he said, "I take it you are a gang leader."

TOO-TALL, I TAKE IT YOU ARE A GANG LEADER.

YEAH. YOU TAKE IT RIGHT.

"Yeah," said Too-Tall. "You take it right."

"Sounds to me as if you're a dictator, Too-Tall. And there are no dictators in a democracy."

Too-Tall yawned. "Who cares about democracy, Mr. Dweeb...I mean, Dweebish?"

Mr. Dweebish didn't bat an eye. He just went right on talking to Too-Tall. "Well, you may not care about democracy, Too-Tall. But democracy cares about you."

"Huh?" said Too-Tall.

"I take it you're not very popular, Too-Tall," said Mr. Dweebish. "Outside of your gang, that is."

Too-Tall didn't answer.

"Most democracies," continued Mr. Dweebish, "protect unpopular people who have unpopular ideas. They protect them from being pushed around by the popular people with popular ideas. That's why the majority doesn't *always* get its way."

Mr. Dweebish looked away from Too-Tall to the whole class. "Suppose Mayor Honeypot, who represents the majority of Bear Country voters, told Too-Tall that he wasn't allowed to say he didn't like democracy. And that if he ever said so again, Chief Bruno would arrest him and throw him in jail. Could that happen?"

"No!" cried Babs Bruno. "My dad would never arrest Too-Tall just for saying something dumb!"

"I'm sure he wouldn't, Ms. Bruno," said Mr. Dweebish. "But Mayor Honeypot wouldn't even be *allowed* to give such an order to Chief Bruno. Because in our Bear Country democracy, we have freedom of speech. Freedom of speech protects us from the majority and the government. It protects us whenever they want to bully us into saying only things that they want to hear."

"Who you callin' a bully?" snapped Too-Tall.

Mr. Dweebish looked at Too-Tall. "No one," he said.

"Oh," said Too-Tall. He was confused. "But you called me unpopular!"

"And I also said it isn't always wrong to

be unpopular," said Mr. Dweebish. "In your case, though, it might be."

"Very funny, Mr. Dweeb," said Too-Tall. "But I don't need to be popular to get my way. If somebody says somethin' I don't like, I pop him. And if somebody takes somethin' that's mine, I pop him and grab it back."

"Aha!" said Mr. Dweebish. He went to the blackboard and wrote on it: "Innocent until proven guilty." He turned back to the

cubs. "Now, we've already talked about the way democracy protects us against bullies who punish people just because of what they say. But Too-Tall just brought up another very important way in which democracy protects us. It's so important, in fact, that it is another foundation of democracy in Bear Country." He pointed to the words on the blackboard.

"Hey, Mr. Dweeb," called Too-Tall.

"It's Dweebish," said the teacher.

"Okay. Dweebish. I don't buy this stuff about innocent until proven guilty. Like I just said, somebody takes somethin' that's mine, I pop him."

"But suppose you didn't see him take it," said Mr. Dweebish.

"No problem," said Too-Tall. "I just figure out who did it. Then I slap him around until he confesses."

"But suppose he didn't do it?" asked the teacher. "Suppose you've got the wrong one?"

Too-Tall thought for a moment. "Who cares?" he said. "All's fair with wimps, nerds, and *dweebs*."

"Oh, will you stop it, Too-Tall," said Brother.

"Yeah," said Cousin Freddy. "Don't be such a jerk."

"Who's gonna make me?" Too-Tall said to Brother. "You and your nerdy little cousin?"

Freddy turned red. He just hated it when Too-Tall called him that! Even though he wasn't nearly as big or as tough as Too-Tall, he jumped up and ran right at the bully. "I told you never to call me that!" he screamed. He swung his fists wildly. But Too-Tall easily held him off with one long,

strong arm. Brother ran after Freddy and tried to pull him away before Too-Tall decided to take a poke at him.

"BACK...IN...YOUR...SEATS!" shouted Mr. Dweebish. "THIS MINUTE!"

"Hey, teacher," said Too-Tall. "I'm already *in* my seat. It's all these wimps and nerds that're runnin' around."

"This time you are right, Too-Tall," said Mr. Dweebish. He glared at the class. "Now, we will all remain quiet and in our seats while I continue my discussion with Too-Tall. If you wish to speak, raise your hand. Understood?"

The cubs all nodded and kept quiet. This Dweebish might be a bit of a nerd. But he was no wimp!

"Now, Too-Tall," said the teacher. "Let's forget about 'innocent until proven guilty' for a moment. Let's talk about why we have a government in the first place. Suppose the cub you thought took your property was bigger than you."

"How much bigger?" asked Too-Tall.

"*Much* bigger."

"No problem, Teach," said Too-Tall. "That's why I've got my gang."

"Right, boss!" said Skuzz, Smirk, and Vinnie all at once.

"And suppose that this really big fellow goes and gets *his* gang," said Mr. Dweebish. "How about that?"

"Yeah," said Brother. "How about that? You and your dumb gangs."

"That's all you ever think about, you big bully," said Babs Bruno. "Gangs and beating people up."

"Of course he'd get his gang!" said Queenie. She was sort of Too-Tall's girl-friend. "What would you expect him to do?"

"But like Mr. Dweebish is saying," said Babs, "then the other guy would get *his* gang. And before you know it, everything is gangs with everybody beating everybody up..."

More cubs joined in. Soon everyone was talking all at once. Usually that bothered the teacher. But Mr. Dweebish didn't look bothered at all. In fact, he was smiling.

He walked to the blackboard again and wrote two more words: "chaos" and "anarchy." He turned to face the class and shouted above the noise, "Chaos—pronounced KAY-oss—means total confusion and disorder. Anarchy—AN-ark-ee—means without law and government...!"

PRONOUNCED KAY-OSS

CHAOS

Suddenly the noise and shouting stopped. There was dead silence in the classroom. Mr. Honeycomb, the principal, was standing in the doorway. And he looked angry.

"Greetings, sir," said Mr. Dweebish. "Welcome to our class in Foundations of Democracy. We were just discussing the

terms 'chaos' and 'anarchy.' "

"It seems to me, Mr. Dweebish," said the principal, "that what you were doing was *demonstrating* the terms 'chaos' and 'anarchy.' "

Again Mr. Dweebish didn't bat an eye. "Well, sir, I guess you're right," he said proudly. "I always like to demonstrate terms and ideas for my students."

"Just try to do it a little more quietly, please," said Mr. Honeycomb. He turned and left the room, closing the door behind him. But by the time he was halfway down the hall to his office, the angry look on his face had disappeared.

Hmm, thought Mr. Honeycomb. We brought this Dweebish fellow in to make social studies more interesting for the students. And noisy or not, he seems to have done that already!

Chapter 3
The Disappearing Baseball Cards

The next day at lunch, Brother, Sister, Freddy, and Lizzy were talking about the new teacher. They had just finished their second class in Foundations of Democracy.

"I like Mr. Dweebish," said Brother. "He isn't boring like the other social studies teachers."

"Yeah," said Sister. "And he lets us DISCUSS."

"I really like the way he goes after Too-Tall," said Freddy.

"As compared to the way *you* went after Too-Tall yesterday?" teased Brother.

"Cool it," said Freddy. "I just lost my temper for a minute."

"Well, you better not let it happen again," said Brother. "I don't think Too-Tall is too happy with the way we've been laughing at him in Mr. Dweebish's class. I have a sneaky feeling that Too-Tall is just waiting for a chance to get back at us."

"And I bet I know who's going to get it first," said Lizzy. "Barry's been laughing at Too-Tall harder than anyone else." Suddenly Lizzy stopped eating. She frowned and looked around the lunchroom. "By the way, where *is* my brother?" she said.

Just then Barry Bruin burst through the double doors of the lunchroom and rushed over to the cubs' table. He was breathing hard. And he had a wild look on his face.

"What's the matter?" asked Lizzy.

"Yeah, what happened?" asked Brother.

"You look like you just lost your favorite thing in the whole world."

"I did!" cried Barry. "A stack of my best baseball cards!" He was near tears.

"Where did you lose them?" asked Freddy.

"I didn't lose them," said Barry. "They were *stolen*!"

"Who did it?" asked Sister.

"I don't know!"

"Where were they stolen?" asked Freddy.

"From my locker," said Barry. "I brought them to school this morning to trade at lunch. I put them in the top part of my locker. They were right under my baseball cap."

"Maybe you left your locker unlocked," said Freddy.

"No," said Barry. "I locked it for sure."

"But nobody can get into a locked locker," said Brother. "Those combination locks are break-in proof. And the combination list is kept in Mr. Honeycomb's office with the test forms and other important secret stuff."

"Maybe you forgot to bring the cards to school this morning," said Lizzy. "You're always forgetting stuff. I'll bet they're at home lying on top of your dresser."

"No way!" said Barry. "I had my Grizzly Koufax and Yogi Grizzwell cards in that stack! I was gonna make a great trade! I'd better go report this to the principal's office."

"Better have some lunch first," said Brother.

Barry looked at Brother with surprise. "Lunch?" he said. "Could *you* eat lunch if *your* Grizzly Koufax card was stolen?"

Brother thought for a moment and shook his head. "You're right," he said. "I probably wouldn't be able to eat for a week."

Barry hurried off to Mr. Honeycomb's office, and the cubs went back to their lunches.

"Who do you think did it?" Sister asked the others.

"I'm still not sure it happened at all," said Lizzy. "I'll bet he just left those cards on his dresser with all the other junk he wants to bring to school and never does."

"But Lizzy," said Freddy, "aren't you forgetting what you said just before Barry came running in?"

"What?" asked Lizzy.

"Don't you remember?" said Brother. "I said that Too-Tall was going to try to get back at us for laughing at him in Mr. Dweebish's class. Then you said Barry would be

the first one to get it because he laughed the hardest."

"Oh, yeah," said Lizzy. "So you think Too-Tall did it?"

"Isn't it obvious?" said Freddy.

"I think it is," said Sister. "But I still don't know what Barry is so upset about. It was just a bunch of stupid baseball cards."

Brother shook his head. "Sis," he said, "how could anyone with as good a fastball as yours not know how much a Grizzly Koufax card means to a guy?"

"Maybe it's because she's not a guy," said Lizzy.

"Shush," said Sister. "I don't need your help with this, Lizzy." She turned back to Brother and said, "Maybe it's because I'm not a guy."

Brother rolled his eyes and leaned back in his chair with a sigh. "Never mind," he said.

Chapter 4
More Thefts

The next day, Brother, Freddy, Lizzy, and Barry sat at their regular lunchroom table. Barry was still upset about his loss.

"Were there any other valuable cards in the group that was stolen?" asked Brother.

"Some okay ones, but Koufax and Grizz-well were my biggies," said Barry. Just then Sister Bear came racing through those very same lunchroom double doors that Barry had burst through. She hurried over to the table where Brother, Freddy, Lizzy, and Barry were sitting.

"There you are," said Lizzy. "We were

just wondering what happened to you. Well, what happened to you?"

Sister was breathing hard and almost ready to cry. She looked just the way Barry had looked the day before.

"I've been ROBBED!" she cried.

Barry's mouth fell open. "You *too?* What did they take?"

"My Bear Scout flashlight! I brought it in for show and tell this afternoon and left it in my locker. And when I went to put my books away at lunchtime, it was gone!"

"That's awful!" said Lizzy.

"Horrible!" said Brother and Freddy.

"Rotten luck," agreed Barry. "But at least it was just a flashlight."

"Just a flashlight?!" cried Sister. "You call an official Bear Scout flashlight JUST A FLASHLIGHT?!"

"Well, it isn't as if it was a Grizzly Koufax baseball card," said Barry.

"It sure isn't!" said Sister. "It's a MIL-LION times more important than some dumb Kizzly Growfax card!"

"Grizzly Koufax," said Barry.

"Quit fighting," said Brother. "This is serious."

"Sure it's serious," said Barry. "But what are we supposed to do?"

"First," said Brother, "Sister should do what Barry did yesterday. She should report the theft to Mr. Honeycomb. Then we'll leave it up to him. He'll know what to do."

The cubs decided to go along with Sister to the principal's office for moral support.

Mr. Honeycomb listened as Sister told him what had happened. When she was finished, he leaned back in his chair and looked up at the ceiling. "Hmm," he said. "That's the second locker theft in two days. I'll have to do something about this."

"Call in Chief Bruno," said Barry Bruin.

"No, I don't think this is serious enough yet for the chief to be bothered," said the principal. "Starting tomorrow morning, we'll set up hall patrols."

As the cubs walked down the hall toward the schoolyard for recess, they discussed their meeting with Mr. Honeycomb.

"Hall patrols," said Freddy. "That might help."

"But why won't he call in the police?" asked Sister. "My Bear Scout flashlight is missing. It's a disaster!"

"And my Grizzly Koufax card!" added

Barry. "That's even more of a disaster!"

"Those may seem like disasters to you guys," said Brother, "but not to Mr. Honeycomb. Let's give him a chance. At least we've got the hall patrols."

But that afternoon, while the hall patrols were still being set up, there were two more thefts. Not only were some baseball cards stolen from Bernie Barr. But a piece of petrified wood that Cousin Freddy had brought in for geology was also missing.

Chapter 5
Guilty or Innocent?

The next morning, Mr. Dweebish started Foundations of Democracy class by asking the cubs what they thought of the locker thefts.

"Rotten. Terrible. Awful," they answered.

"I understand that Mr. Honeycomb has set up hall patrols," said Mr. Dweebish. "Is that a good idea?"

Babs Bruno raised her hand. "Sure it's a good idea," she said. "But it's not enough."

"How would you handle this problem, Babs?" asked Mr. Dweebish.

"I'd bring in my dad and Officer Marguerite. And I'd have them search every cub and locker in the school. And that would be the end of it."

"Yes," said Mr. Dweebish, "that might well be the end of it. But wouldn't it also be the end of privacy in Bear Country School?"

Sister raised her hand. "I don't buy that privacy stuff, Mr. Dweebish," she said. "Chief Bruno can search my locker any time he feels like it. I don't need privacy, because I've got nothing to hide."

But some of the other cubs were already thinking about things in their lockers that they wanted to keep private. The trouble was, they didn't want to talk about their private things in class.

Finally, Queenie McBear came to the rescue. "I disagree with Sister," she said bravely. "Sometimes I keep my diary in my locker. And my diary is *my* business and nobody else's."

"Now *there's* something worth stealing!" said Too-Tall. Queenie pretended to give him a nasty look. Then she winked at him. Too-Tall grinned and winked back.

"Queenie made a very good point," said Mr. Dweebish. "In our Bear Country democracy people have a right to privacy. That's one of the rules that are the foundations of democracy. The police can't search everyone just because they feel like it."

"They don't need to search everyone," said Babs. "Just Too-Tall. Because we all know he's the thief."

"Aw, come off it, Babs," groaned Too-Tall. "What would I want with a stupid flashlight and a nerdy piece of petrified wood?"

"My flashlight isn't stupid!" cried Sister.

"And don't call me nerdy!" Freddy yelled.

"I didn't call *you* nerdy," said Too-Tall with a laugh. "I called your *wood* nerdy."

"Quiet!" said Mr. Dweebish in a firm voice. "I think it's time we return to something we discussed the other day." He went to the blackboard, picked up a piece of

chalk, and wrote once more: "Innocent until proven guilty."

The cubs all groaned. "Not again," said Barry.

"Now wait a minute," said Mr. Dweebish. "A few days ago, you all seemed to like the idea of 'innocent until proven guilty.' That was when I argued with Too-Tall about it. But now I'm using it to protect Too-Tall. And suddenly you don't like it anymore! What's going on here, class?"

Freddy spoke up. "What's going on, Mr. Dweebish, is that we all know that Too-Tall and the gang are the thieves."

"How do you know that?" asked Mr.

Dweebish. "Isn't Too-Tall right when he says that he has no reason to steal a flashlight and a piece of petrified wood?"

"But he does have a reason," said Brother. "He wants to get back at us for laughing at him in class."

"And it wasn't just a flashlight and petrified wood that he took," said Barry. "He took baseball cards too. And we all know how much Too-Tall loves baseball cards. He's got one of the best collections in Bear Country."

"That's right!" said Too-Tall. "So why would I want your crummy Grizzly Koufax and Yogi Grizzwell cards? I've got five of each already!"

"Maybe you wanted SIX of each!" said Barry.

"Yeah!" said Sister. "And you've been mixed up in most of the other trouble here

at school ever since I can remember!"

"Calm down, class," said Mr. Dweebish.
"These are all interesting questions and
arguments. But they don't *prove* anything.

"The fact that Too-Tall and the gang have been in trouble before doesn't mean they're guilty this time. And the fact that some of you think Too-Tall wants to get back at you doesn't mean that he really does. And even if he really does want to, he may not have done anything about it yet.

"What I'm hearing from you cubs is just a lot of interesting ideas and opinions. To prove that Too-Tall is guilty, you need more than that. You need...what's the word I'm looking for, class?"

Queenie's hand shot up. "Evidence," she said.

"Exactly," said Mr. Dweebish.

"That's my girl!" said Too-Tall. "You tell 'em, Queenie!"

Too-Tall had the last word in Foundations of Democracy that day. Because just then the bell rang for lunch.

Chapter 6
Grizzmeyer Grills the Gang

The hall patrols didn't seem to be doing much good. More lockers were robbed over the next few days. No one had a clue as to who was doing it or how it was being done. All kinds of things were stolen. A special comb with gold trim was stolen from Lizzy Bruin's locker. An arrowhead was taken from Gil Grizzwold's locker. And more baseball cards were stolen.

The school's vice principal, Mr. Grizzmeyer, had a theory about the locker thefts. He was Too-Tall's baseball coach and knew all about how much Too-Tall loved baseball cards. So he believed that Too-Tall, or one of his gang, was stealing the cards. And he figured that Too-Tall was stealing other things so that people would think someone else was the thief. Mr. Grizzmeyer decided it was time to talk to Too-Tall and the gang about the thefts.

Too-Tall and the gang were shown into the principal's office. They were not surprised to find Mr. Grizzmeyer there standing beside Mr. Honeycomb.

"Hi, Coach," said Too-Tall.

"Just sit down," snapped Mr. Grizzmeyer.

"Sure, Coach," the gang said all together.

They sat in chairs in front of the principal's desk.

"Now, cubs," said Mr. Honeycomb. "We've called you here to discuss a very serious matter..."

"Excuse me, sir," said Mr. Grizzmeyer, "but these guys know *exactly* why they're here."

"We do?" said Too-Tall. He looked at his gang with big question marks in his eyes. "Do *you* know, Skuzz?"

"I dunno, boss," said Skuzz.

"Do *you* know, Smirk?"

"I dunno, boss..."

"Enough of that!" barked Mr. Grizz-meyer. "Just tell us how you've been doing it."

"Doin' *what*?" asked Too-Tall. He turned again to Skuzz. "Do you know what he's talkin' about?"

"I dunno, boss..."

"I SAID COOL IT!" roared Grizzmeyer. "We know you guys have been robbing lock-ers!"

"US?" said Too-Tall with a gasp. "How do you know that?"

"Because you guys are *always* at the bot-tom of these stunts," said Mr. Grizzmeyer.

"*Always?*" said Too-Tall. "What about the time Gil Grizzwold dumped a can of trash all over Miss Glitch's car?"

"Nice try, Too-Tall," said Mr. Grizzmeyer. "We also know you love baseball cards. And that you want to get back at the cubs for laughing at you in class..."

"Now wait just a minute, Mr. G," said Too-Tall. He held up a hand. "I've been listenin' real careful to Mr. Dweeb—er, Dweebish—in Foundations of Democracy, and I know you need more than that to prove me guilty."

"That's enough back talk, Too-Tall!" growled Mr. Grizzmeyer.

"It ain't back talk, Mr. G," said Too-Tall sweetly. "It's a *foundation of democracy.* Right, guys?"

The gang members nodded.

"Innocent until proven guilty," said Too-Tall. "And with all due respect, Mr. G and Mr. H, you ain't proven me guilty yet. 'Cause you ain't got no..."

Too-Tall turned to his gang with a puzzled look. "What was that word Queenie used in Dweeb's class the other day?"

"I dunno, boss," said Skuzz.

Smirk shrugged. "I forget, boss."

Vinnie leaned across and whispered something in Too-Tall's ear.

"That's it," said Too-Tall. "You ain't got no EVIDENCE!"

Mr. Grizzmeyer's face was red with fury. "Why, I'll have you all suspended...!" he yelled.

But Mr. Honeycomb held up his hand to stop Mr. Grizzmeyer. With a tired look, he

said, "I'm afraid Too-Tall's right, Mr. Grizzmeyer. We ain't got no evidence. I mean, we DON'T got no evidence...I mean, we don't HAVE no evidence...I mean, we don't have ANY evidence! *Phew!*"

The way Mr. Grizzmeyer set his jaw when he was angry made him look a lot like a bulldog. "All right!" he barked at the gang. "Outta my sight! NOW!"

When the gang had gone, Mr. Grizzmeyer turned to the principal and said, "We should suspend those bums anyway."

Mr. Honeycomb just smiled. "Suspend the whole gang during baseball season, Mr. Grizzmeyer? What would you do for a catcher? And a first baseman, and a third baseman, and a center fielder?"

Mr. Grizzmeyer's frown turned into a silly grin. "Just kidding, Mr. H," he said.

Chapter 7
The Bear Detectives
Rise Again!

"Hey," said Cousin Freddy to Brother and Sister Bear as they walked home from school that afternoon. "Did you hear what happened when Mr. H and Mr. G grilled Too-Tall and the gang today?"

"What?" asked Brother.

"Too-Tall told them he was innocent until proven guilty and that they didn't have any evidence. And they let him go!" Freddy couldn't help laughing. "Is that great or what?"

Everyone laughed along. When the laughter died down, Brother said, "It's funny. But it's not funny too. Mr. G is right. Too-Tall is stealing baseball cards. And he's trying to make it look like somebody else is doing it by stealing other stuff too."

"But Too-Tall is right too," said Sister. "Nobody's got any evidence."

The cubs walked along in silence for a while. Suddenly Sister got a funny look in her eyes and stopped. She was lost in thought. Brother and Freddy stopped too. "What is it?" asked Freddy.

"Evidence," said Sister. "We need evidence. And who collects evidence?"

"Uh...laboratory scientists?" said Freddy.

"No, dummy!" said Sister. "Evidence about crimes!"

"Detectives," said Brother.

"Right," said Sister. "So who should collect the evidence about the locker thefts at Bear Country School? Come on, guys. Use those high-powered brains!"

Brother's face lit up. "Of course!" he cried. "The Bear Detectives!"

"Right!" said Freddy. "The Bear Detectives rise again! But where do we start?"

It was a good question. The would-be detectives sat down by the side of the road to think. Minutes passed before Sister had the first bright idea. "Let's break into Too-Tall's locker," she said.

"Bad idea," said Brother. "We'd be criminals ourselves. Besides, we'd never be able to break into his locker. Not even with a crowbar."

"Maybe we could get the combination," said Freddy.

"It would still be a crime," said Brother. "Besides, that's the most mysterious part of the mystery. Those combinations are under lock and key in the principal's office. And anyway, the evidence might not be in the locker."

The cubs sat and thought some more.

"How 'about this?" Sister said after a while. "Let's *shadow* Too-Tall and the gang. You know, follow them like real detectives."

"Hmm," said Brother.

"We'd have to make sure they didn't see us," said Freddy.

"What do you think we could find out?" asked Sister.

"Who knows?" said Brother. "Maybe they're sneaking into school after it's closed."

"Maybe they'll lead us to where they've hidden the stolen goods," said Freddy.

"Okay," said Brother. "We've been sitting and thinking long enough. *Let's do it!* We'll drop off our books. Then we'll pick up Too-Tall and his gang at Biff Bruin's pharmacy. I'm sure they'll be there. That's where they always hang out. And Freddy, bring your bird-watching binoculars. Because these birds are going to need some heavy-duty watching!"

Sure enough, Too-Tall and the gang were in their regular booth at the pharmacy.

"Just act cool," said Brother. "Act like we're here to buy stuff."

But it was hard to act cool around Too-Tall.

"I'm innocent! I'm innocent!" he screamed when he saw Brother, Freddy, and Sister. He flopped out of the booth onto the floor. "Please don't beat me! Please don't throw me into that burning fire!"

"Just ignore him," said Brother.

"He's pretty hard to ignore rolling around on the floor and screaming like that," said Sister. She was pretending to read a comic book.

Biff Bruin came running out from the back room, where he was working on a pre-scription. "What's going on here?" he said.

Too-Tall got to his feet and brushed him-self off. "It's okay, Biff," he said. "I was just explaining the foundations of democracy to these cubs. Especially one called INNO-CENT UNTIL PROVEN GUILTY!"

"It's okay, Mr. Bruin," said Brother. "We're leaving."

They could hear Too-Tall and the gang howling with laughter as they left the pharmacy. Sister was steaming. "He makes me so mad!" she yelled.

"Take it easy, Sis," said Brother. "This is working out perfectly."

"How so?" asked Freddy.

"We'll just act like we're heading home," said Brother. "Once we're around the corner, we'll duck into the bushes. They'll never guess we're planning to shadow them."

"Hey, that's right!" said Sister.

They found a spot with a good view of Biff's. Then they ducked down and waited for Too-Tall and his gang to come out.

"They're coming out!" said Freddy. "Let's go!"

"Not so fast," said Brother. He held Freddy and Sister back. "Don't let them see us, or the whole thing will be a waste."

The Bear Detectives followed Too-Tall and the gang at a safe distance. They kept well out of sight.

"Look!" said Sister. "They're headed for the Burger Bear!"

"So?" said Brother. "There's nothing suspicious about the Burger Bear."

"You never know," said Freddy. He looked through his binoculars at the Burger Bear's big front window. "Aha!" he cried.

"What are they doing?" said Sister.

"They're...drinking milk shakes," said Freddy.

"Drinking milk shakes?" said Brother. "That's not 'aha!' That's 'ho-hum.'"

Suddenly Freddy cried, "Get down! Quick!"

The cubs ducked down out of sight. "What's wrong?" asked Sister.

"They just looked in our direction," said Freddy.

"But do you think they saw us?" asked Brother. Freddy poked the binoculars through the bushes. "Well?" said Brother. "DO YOU THINK THEY SAW US?"

"I don't think so," said Freddy after a while. "It's just that the binoculars make them seem so close. So when they looked over here, I got scared. Wait. They're coming out. Get ready to follow."

"Uh-oh," said Brother. "They're splitting up!"

"What'll we do?" cried Sister.

"*We'll* split up," said Brother. "I'll take Too-Tall, Freddy will take Skuzz. Sister, you take Smirk..."

"*What about Vinnie?*" said Sister.

"Hey," said Brother, "sometimes you have to work shorthanded. Now *let's go!*"

Chapter 8
The Bear Detectives
on the Trail

The Bear Detectives did their best following the gang whenever it split up. But their best didn't seem to be good enough. Two days later, there was another school-locker theft. The Bear Detectives met at afternoon recess to talk about it.

"That could mean that Vinnie is the thief," said Sister. "He's the one we haven't followed yet."

"Right," said Brother. "After school I'll take Vinnie instead of Too-Tall if the gang splits up."

But that afternoon the gang didn't split

up. From school they headed straight into
some nearby woods. The Bear Detectives
had no trouble keeping up with them. That
was because Too-Tall was carrying something. *He was carrying a heavy box that
slowed the gang down.*

The cubs made their way along a narrow
trail through the trees. "What do you think
is in the box?" whispered Sister.

"*The stolen goods,* what else?" Freddy
whispered back.

"Yeah," said Brother. "I think we've
finally got 'em."

The gang stopped at an old hollow tree and set the box down on the ground. The Bear Detectives hid in some bushes. It was hard to see clearly through all the leaves. Even Freddy's binoculars didn't help very much.

"What are they doing?" asked Sister.

"I'm not sure," said Freddy. "Wait...Too-Tall's picking up the box... Yes! He's hiding it in the hollow of that old tree!"

"All right!" said Brother. "Now we've got 'em for sure!"

The cubs waited silently until the gang left. Then they hurried to the old tree. Brother reached into the hollow and lifted out the cardboard box. It wasn't so heavy after all. "Doesn't feel like baseball cards," he said. He shook it a little.

"Come on, open it," said Freddy. He tried to grab the box.

Brother jerked the box away. "Hold your horses, Freddy!"

But Freddy was so excited he couldn't wait. He grabbed one of the box's flaps and yanked. The contents spilled out all over the three cubs' feet. They looked down. It wasn't stolen goods. It was...

"GARBAGE!" the cubs cried out.

And that's exactly what it was. Old cans, orange and banana peels, plastic wrappers, and eggshells were lying all over the place.

Suddenly Too-Tall and the gang leapt out from behind some bushes and shouted, "GARBAGE! That's what your evidence is! GARBAGE!" Then they laughed wildly and ran off through the woods. And they left the Bear Detectives with egg on their faces and garbage on their feet.

Chapter 9
To the Thinking Place

Nothing in the world is worse than chasing after evidence and finding only garbage. It's especially bad when the garbage winds up all over your feet with the criminals laughing at you.

It was pretty clear what had happened. Too-Tall and the gang *had* seen the cubs back at the Burger Bear. Maybe Freddy's binoculars glinting in the sun had given them away. Or maybe Too-Tall had figured it out as soon as they walked into Biff's pharmacy. But it really didn't matter. What did matter was that the idea of shadowing the locker thieves hadn't worked. It was a bust. A complete bust.

The Bear Detectives knew that they needed to talk things over. They needed to make a new plan for proving the gang guilty. Brother's Thinking Place was not far from the old hollow tree. This was the rocky spot in the woods where Brother went whenever he had to think things over.

The cubs sat on some rocks at the Thinking Place and thought hard.

After a while Sister spoke up. "I just thought of something," she said. "Except for Too-Tall and his gang, Brother is the only member of the Foundations of Democracy

class who hasn't been robbed yet."

"Hey, you're right," said Freddy.

"They wouldn't rob themselves," said Brother. "But then again, they might. Just to throw everyone off the trail."

"Yes, but they haven't," said Sister.

Brother kept thinking. His Thinking Place hadn't failed him yet. And he didn't want this to be the first time.

"So," said Brother, "the big question is, why haven't *I* been robbed yet?"

"Wrong," said Freddy. "It doesn't matter why. That's because we can use it to catch Too-Tall. Here's what we do. First we rig up a trap in Brother's locker. Then we spread the word that Too-Tall won't rob Brother's locker because he's yellow-chicken-just-plain-scared of Brother. As soon as Too-Tall hears that, a machine gun couldn't keep him away from Brother's locker."

"But who's gonna believe that?" asked Brother. "Too-Tall's not scared of me. Everybody knows that."

"But you *did* dump him in the mall Dumpster when both of you wanted to take Bonnie Brown to the Spring Dance," Freddy pointed out. "We'll say he's been scared of you ever since."

Brother thought for a moment. "It just might work," he said. Suddenly his eyes lit up. "*Especially* if I say that I'm going to bring my Babe Bruin rookie card to school to trade. And that I'm going to keep it in my locker!"

"Perfect," said Freddy. "Now listen, guys. First we visit Bonnie Brown's uncle, Squire Grizzly. He's the president of the Great Grizzly National Bank. The bank uses paint bombs to catch robbers. I'll bet he can help us rig up a paint bomb in Brother's locker.

Then, when Too-Tall opens the door to steal that Babe Bruin card—SPLATTO! We'll catch him red-handed!"

"Yeah!" said Sister. "And red-faced and red-chested and red-everything-else!"

Chapter 10
The Mad Bombers
of Bear Country School

Squire Grizzly was a bank president. So naturally he hated robbers more than anything. He was more than happy to help the Bear Detectives with their scheme. Early the next morning, the Squire sent one of his security men to Bear Country School to rig up a red paint bomb in Brother's locker.

As the Bear Detectives made their way down the hall to class that morning, they passed the locker. It looked just like all the others. There was no sign that a trap had been set. Quickly, the cubs spread the word that Brother's Babe Bruin card was in the locker and that Too-Tall was afraid of Brother.

"All we have to do now," said Sister, "is wait for Too-Tall or one of the gang to show up in class with red paint all over him."

"Great," said Brother. "Let me put my jacket away." Brother already had a hand on his combination lock.

"Stop!" cried Freddy.

"Huh?" said Brother.

"Haven't you forgotten something?" asked Freddy.

Brother frowned. Then he grinned foolishly. "Oh, yeah...heh heh...the paint bomb," he said. "My locker looks so normal it even had *me* fooled."

The cubs hurried off to class and waited for the gang to show up. But when they arrived, a few minutes late as usual, not one of them was red-faced. And not one of them was red-faced after lunch or after afternoon recess, either. By the end of the school day, Brother's locker had not been opened by anyone!

"Aha!" said Brother. The cubs stood in front of his locker. "They're not doing it during school anymore. They're doing it *after* school. Or maybe even at night."

"So what do we do?" asked Sister.

"Simple," said Brother. "We go home and forget about it. When we come back to school tomorrow morning, the trap will be sprung. And my locker will be covered with red paint."

"And so will one of the gang," said Freddy.

The cubs went home and tried to forget about the paint bomb. But it was hard not to think about it. They just couldn't wait to see Too-Tall or one of the gang all covered with red paint.

And sure enough, when the cubs arrived at school the next morning, Brother's locker was wide open. And it was splattered all over with red paint.

"Yahoo!" cried Brother. "We finally got 'em!"

"I can't wait for Too-Tall to get here!" said Sister.

"Be patient, Sis," said Brother. "I've been thinking about this. It seems to me that Too-Tall, or whichever gang member did it, isn't stupid enough to come to school covered with the evidence. At morning recess,

we'll go to Mr. Honeycomb and tell him what we did. Then he can call Chief Bruno, who can go pick up the gang."

"I don't think we'll need to do that," said Freddy.

"Why not?" asked Brother.

Freddy pointed down the hall. "Because here come Too-Tall and the gang right now."

Brother and Sister turned to look. Too-Tall, Skuzz, Smirk, and Vinnie were walking calmly down the hall to Teacher Bob's class. And there wasn't a speck of red paint on any of them.

"They washed it off already!" cried Sister.

"No way," said Freddy. "That stuff is unwashable. It would take days to get it off."

The gang passed the cubs. Too-Tall noticed Brother's locker and stopped. "Hey, guys, look at this," he said with a laugh. "What happened to your locker, Brother?"

"Paint bomb," said Brother.

"Cool!" said Too-Tall. "But you didn't get hit."

"Neither did you, I see," said Brother.

"Me?" said Too-Tall. He sounded puzzled. "I don't get it."

"Neither do I," said Brother.

"Hey, guys," Too-Tall said to the gang. "Do you know what he's talkin' about?"

"I dunno, boss," said Skuzz.

"Beats me," said Smirk.

"I think Brother's gone wacko," suggested Vinnie.

"Well," said Too-Tall, "it sure wasn't me who broke into that locker, gang. Remember, I'm yellow-chicken-just-plain-scared of big bad Brother Bear! BAWK BAWK BAWK BAWK!"

The gang laughed loudly and strutted off down the hall doing chicken-wings with their elbows. The cubs were left shaking their heads.

Chapter 11
Caught Red-Handed

The Bear Detectives had trouble paying attention in class that morning. They couldn't get their minds off the red-handed thief. Who was it? Whoever it was surely wouldn't come to school today. But all the cubs in Teacher Bob's class were there! Was it someone from outside class? Maybe even someone from outside school?

Finally, it was time for Foundations of Democracy. Teacher Bob looked at his watch and asked for the cubs' attention. "I have an important announcement, class," he said. "There will be no Foundations of

Democracy today. This is a free period."

The cubs all groaned. They liked Foundations of Democracy. It was fun and exciting.

But one cub didn't groan. He was too busy thinking. Brother Bear looked up at the blackboard at what Mr. Dweebish had written in the corner the day before. "Innocent until proven guilty." It was the third or fourth time Mr. Dweebish had written that on the board. And this time he had asked Teacher Bob not to erase it. The social studies teacher was certainly trying hard to get that idea across. Maybe, thought Brother, a little *too* hard...

When the bell rang for lunch, Sister and Cousin Freddy headed toward the lunchroom as usual. But Brother stopped them in the hall. "We're not going to the lunchroom today," he said.

"Speak for yourself," said Sister. "I'm hungry."

"We're going to Miz McGrizz's house instead," said Brother. He walked swiftly to the front door. Sister and Freddy hurried after him.

"But I don't want to have lunch with Miz McGrizz," whined Sister.

"Not for lunch," said Brother.

"For Bear Detectives work?" asked Freddy.

"Yup," said Brother. "I have a feeling we'll find our red-handed thief there."

"Miz McGrizz?" said Sister. "You've gotta be kidding!"

"I'm not kidding," said Brother. "But I *don't* mean Miz McGrizz."

"Oh!" said Freddy. "You mean—"

"That's right," said Brother. "Mr. Dweebish is boarding with Miz McGrizz. And he didn't come to school today!"

The cubs hurried to Miz McGrizz's house and rang the doorbell. Kindly old Miz McGrizz opened the door and smiled down at them. "Well, what a pleasant surprise!" she said. "What can I do for you cubs?"

"We have to see Mr. Dweebish," said Brother.

Miz McGrizz looked back toward the stairs. "I'm afraid Mr. Dweebish hasn't come down from his room yet," she said. "Perhaps..."

"I'm here," said a loud clear voice coming down the stairs. "Let them come in, Miz McGrizz."

Miz McGrizz showed the cubs into the living room. Mr. Dweebish was already sitting in a comfy chair. But he didn't look very comfortable. His face was all red. So were his ears, his hands, his knees, and his everything else.

Sister was shocked. "But *why,* Mr. Dwee-bish?" she asked. "Why did you do it?"

Mr. Dweebish let out a big sigh. "Guess," he said.

"I know," said Brother. "Innocent until proven guilty. Right?"

"Smart cub," said Mr. Dweebish. "I wanted to show Too-Tall what it's like to be accused of a crime he didn't commit. I thought that might give him more respect for democracy. And I also wanted to teach the rest of you a lesson—a lesson about accusing someone of committing a crime just because he's unpopular and has been in trouble before.

"Today, in Foundations of Democracy, I was going to tell everyone about my experi-ment and give back all the stolen goods to their owners. I never expected *this* to hap-pen." He held up his red hands.

"Wow," said Sister. "I'll bet Mr. Honey-comb is really mad at you. And Mr. Grizzmeyer too. You sent them on a wild goose chase. And come to think of it, you invaded cubs' privacy too. And you stole stuff! I thought I'd never see my Bear Scout flashlight again!"

"Shhh," whispered Brother. "The poor guy feels dumb enough already." Then he said, "There's something I've been wonder-ing about, Mr. Dweebish. How did you get the combinations?"

"Simple," said the red-faced teacher. "I just told Mr. Honeycomb I needed to see the social studies quizzes they'd been using. He gave me the key. I took the combinations list, copied it, then put it back under lock and key."

"Way out!" said Freddy.

"Way out of *line,* you mean," said Mr. Dweebish. He might have been blushing. But who could tell? "Sister is absolutely right. I invaded privacy. I committed crimes. I broke the rules. I did all the things I've been telling you cubs in Foundations of Democracy *not* to do. All because of a silly experiment. I let my love of demonstrating ideas to my students get the best of me."

"Probably not the first time," Brother whispered to Freddy.

"Or the last," Freddy whispered back.

"Anyway," continued Mr. Dweebish, "I'm very sorry indeed for all the trouble I've caused. Tomorrow I'm going back to the

University. I don't think anyone at Bear Country School will trust me after this. I'll turn all the stolen goods over to Mr. Honeycomb. He'll see that they get to their owners."

"Mr. Dweebish?" said Sister. "If it isn't too much trouble, would you give me my flashlight right now?"

"And my petrified wood?" asked Freddy.

"Cool it, guys," said Brother. "Let's leave him alone. You'll get your stuff soon enough."

The cubs said good-bye to Mr. Dweebish and wished him luck at the university. Then they headed back to school. By now their stomachs were grumbling from hunger.

Mr. Dweebish did indeed go back to Bear Country University the next day. And the cubs did get back their stolen goods. Everything at Bear Country School returned to normal. More or less. And soon the cubs of Teacher Bob's class forgot all about the trouble caused by Mr. Dweebish, The Red-Handed Thief.

But they never forgot two very important lessons from Foundations of Democracy. The first was that social studies doesn't have to be boring. And the second was that in Bear Country, everyone is innocent until proven guilty.

Even Too-Tall Grizzly.

Stan and Jan Berenstain began writing and illustrating books for children in the early 1960s, when their two young sons were beginning to read. That marked the start of the best-selling Berenstain Bears series. Now, with more than 95 books in print, videos, television shows, and even Berenstain Bears attractions at major amusement parks, it's hard to tell where the Bears end and the Berenstains begin!

Stan and Jan make their home in Bucks County, Pennsylvania, near their sons—Leo, a writer, and Michael, an illustrator—who are helping them with Big Chapter Books stories and pictures. They plan on writing and illustrating many more books for children, especially for their four grandchildren, who keep them well in touch with the kids of today.